Barbie™

Barbie Loves Springtime

Barbie™

Barbie Loves Springtime

Barbie loves spring. It's such a wonderful time of year!
The shining sun feels warm, and the cool breeze blows her hair.

In the spring, Barbie loves to spend her time outside taking long walks and bicycle rides through the park.
Barbie takes a deep breath. The fresh-cut grass in the park smells great!

There are pretty colours everywhere! Barbie can't believe her eyes. The sky is filled with butterflies and flying kites. Pinks, oranges, greens and blues flutter in the wind.

Barbie gets on her bicycle and pedals down the path.
As she rides along, Barbie sees many people enjoying the beautiful
spring day. They are having such a good time.

Barbie finds a field filled with blooming wild flowers.
She takes off her shoes and feels the beautiful flowers tickling her toes.

Barbie joins her friends for a picnic. The food tastes delicious!
Barbie tosses leftover bread crumbs to the quacking ducks.
They swim all round the pond to catch the food.

Barbie loves spring because it's the perfect season for everyone to be outdoors!

Springtime Games

Play this game with a friend. Use small buttons as counters and use a coin to move spaces.
Move one space for heads and three spaces for tails.
The first person to finish wins!

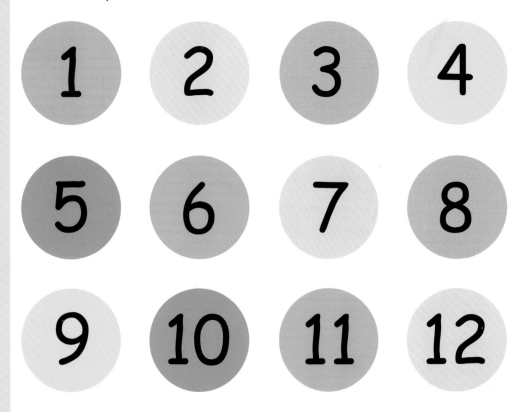

13	14	15	16
17	18	19	20
21	22	23	24
25	26	27	28

S-s-s-s-s-s-spring!

Barbie loves spring! Use some of the 's' words below to finish these surprising springtime sentences!

Write them in pencil so that when you've finished you can rub them out and make up some more.

Barbie's _____ is/are _____ and _____ .

Barbie _____ a _____ .

Barbie loves _____ .

In the blank lines below make up new sentences using as many 's' words as possible.

_____

_____

_____

_____

_____

_____

sees	supposes	sweet	sandcastle
sings	sells	super	starfish
sails	seeks	strong	ship
says	sunny	small	shell
shows	scary	slow	shirt
swims	smelly	surprising	sky
skates	silly	sand	spade
skips	shiny	soap	spectacle
speaks	special	song	strawberry

Colouring Kites

Colour in these kites. Look at the pictures in the story if you need some help.

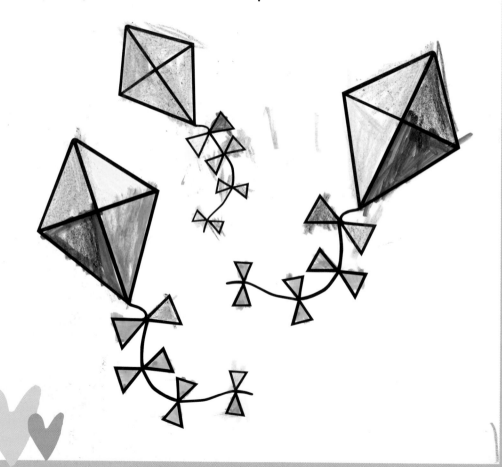

First published in Great Britain 1998
This edition published 2001 by Egmont Children's Books Limited
a division of Egmont Holding Limited
239 Kensington High Street, London W8 6SA

Copyright © 2001 Mattel, Inc. All Rights Reserved.
Originally published in USA by Golden Books Limited.
BARBIE and associated trademarks are owned by and used under licence from Mattel, Inc.

ISBN 0 434 80766 4

Printed in China

1 3 5 7 9 10 8 6 4 2